in the RAINFOREST

BY
BARBARA TAYLOR

THE LIVING FOREST

Imagine walking through a warm, damp, dark forest with huge trees forming a green roof that shuts out the sky. The buzzing of insects fills the air and occasionally you glimpse a bird or a monkey high in the treetops. This is what a rainforest is like. At least half of all the animal and plant species in the world live in rainforests. There are at least 30 million different insects alone. The main reasons for this incredible richness are the warm, wet climate all year round and the constant competition to find living space and avoid predators. People often call rainforests "jungles," from the Hindi "jangal," meaning the thick forest that grows after the original forest is cleared.

CANOPY CREATURES

In the busy, bustling world of the canopy, the tree branches form a convenient high-level walkway used by many animals, such as this howler monkey. Fruit bats and birds fly through the leaves and branches.

LAYERS OF LIFE

A rainforest can be divided into four main layers.

THE EMERGENT LAYER
Some giant trees, called emergents, grow beyond the top floor of the forest.

THE CANOPY
Most rainforest life is found in the canopy, some 130 ft (40 meters) above the ground. This layer receives the most rain and sunshine, and so contains the most food, such as leaves, flowers, and fruits.

THE UNDERSTORY
Between the canopy and the forest floor is an understory of smaller trees, climbing plants, and large-leaved shrubs that can tolerate the shade.

THE FOREST FLOOR
Only one or two percent of the sunlight that hits the canopy filters through to the forest floor. The ground is almost bare except for a thin carpet of leaves.

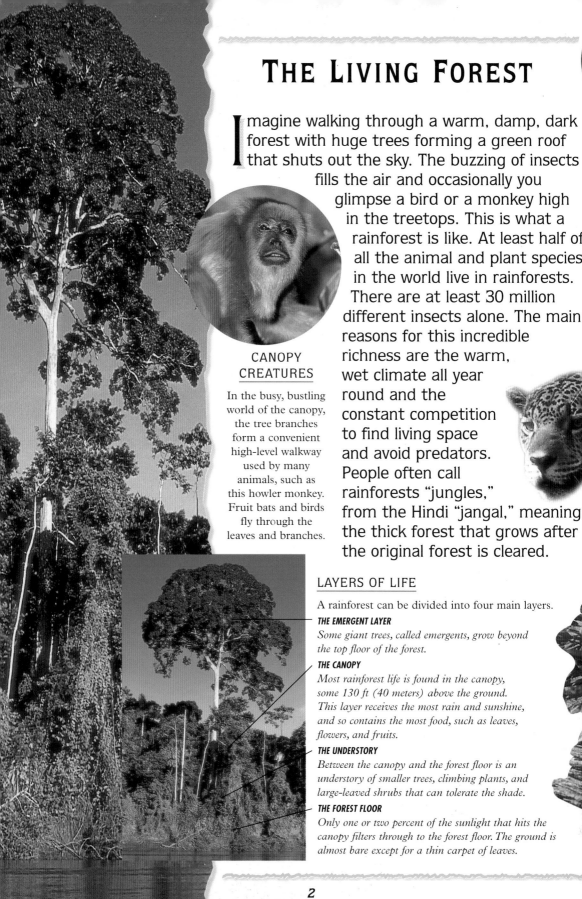

FOREST GIANTS

The year-round warmth of the rainforest has allowed some animals to grow into giants, such as the giant millipedes. These look rather alarming, but actually feed on dead plant material. Other rainforest giants include the largest frog in the world, the goliath frog, and the largest butterfly, the Queen Alexandra's birdwing butterfly.

FOREST PEOPLE

This Kalapolo Indian lives in the Brazilian rainforest. People have inhabited rainforests for thousands of years, but little is known of their origins, their relationship to one another, or how they colonized the forest. Warmth and moisture break down organic materials, such as wood, very quickly, so ancient remains are rare.

LIFE IN THE UNDERSTORY

Among the tangle of leaves and branches in the understory live climbing and grasping animals. Many are small and light, such as tree frogs, lemurs, coatis, and tree snakes like this emerald tree boa. Others are much heavier and have to keep to the larger branches.

THE FOREST FLOOR

Large hunters such as jaguars and tigers prowl along the forest floor. Hogs, peccaries, and tapirs can root out bulbs and shoots from the soil, and there are plenty of insects for hungry giant anteaters and tenrecs.

RAINFORESTS OF THE WORLD

WHERE IN THE WORLD?

There are four main areas of rainforest in the world today – in Central and South America, in Africa, in Southeast Asia, and in Australasia shaded dark green. Every rainforest in the world is different with many species of plants and animals living only in one area. This is because the continents have drifted apart over millions of years, separating the different areas of rainforest so that the plants and animals developed separately into different forms.

The word "rain" forest was first used in 1898 to describe forests that grow in constantly wet conditions. Most rainforests have an annual rainfall of almost 100 inches (250 cm), which is spread evenly throughout the year. Thunderstorms are common in the afternoons. Water given off by the trees adds to the moisture in the air, so the air feels sticky, or humid, and clouds and mist hang over the forest like smoke. This blanket of cloud protects the forest from daytime heat and nighttime chill, keeping temperatures between 73°F (23°C) and 88°F (31°C) throughout the year. The hottest, wettest rainforests occur in a narrow belt around the Equator. These are sometimes called lowland rainforests and they are the most extensive. Rainforests further away from the Equator are just as warm as lowland rainforests, but have a short dry season. Another type of rainforest, called cloud forest, grows on tropical mountains, while mangrove rainforests grow on some tropical coasts.

COLD AIR

WARM AIR

EQUATOR

TROPICAL RAIN

Rainforests are wet because they grow in a band around the middle of the Earth where the sun's rays are at their hottest and strongest. The sun's heat warms the ground, which then warms the air above it. The warm air rises up. As it rises, it cools down and moisture in the air condenses into water droplets, which collect to make clouds and rain.

MONSOON OR SEASONAL FORESTS

Tropical rainforests with three or more dry months each year are called monsoon forests or seasonal forests. This is because the trees drop their leaves in the dry season and grow new leaves at the start of the wet monsoon season. These forests have fewer climbing plants than lowland rainforests because the air is drier. There are also more plants growing on the forest floor because a lot of light reaches the ground in the dry season.

CLOUD FORESTS

High up on tropical mountains – above 3,000 ft (900 meters) – grow misty forests of gnarled, twisted, stunted trees covered in bright green mosses and dripping with water. Lichens hang down like beards from the tree branches and ferns, orchids, and other plants perch along the boughs. These cloud (or montane) forests have fewer plant species than lowland forests, as low temperatures and strong winds restrict plant growth.

MANGROVE FORESTS

Tropical shorelines are often clothed in a special type of rainforest, called a mangrove forest, which does not have a great variety of species. These forests grow on the coasts of the Indian Ocean, the western Pacific Ocean, and also on the shores of Central and South America, the Caribbean, and West Africa.

WHAT'S THE WEATHER?

Inside a rainforest, the local, or micro-climate, varies at different levels. Animals on the forest floor experience different conditions than those in the canopy. When it rains, the water drips down through the leaves, sometimes taking 10 minutes to reach the ground. When the sun shines, the air at the top of the canopy is hot and dry, but on the ground it is always warm and damp. A strong wind may be blowing up in the canopy, but at ground level there isn't even a breeze.

THE WATER CYCLE

As rain drips down through the rainforest, the trees and plants take in moisture through their leaves and roots. Unused water evaporates, or disappears, into the air through tiny holes in their leaves. Water also evaporates from the ground. All the warm, wet air rises up into the sky, where it cools down to make rain clouds. Rain falls down from the clouds into the forest to start the rainfall cycle all over again.

ASIAN RAINFORESTS

The main area of rainforest in Southeast Asia spreads down the mainland of Malaysia to Indonesia. Widespread human disturbance of the forests of mainland Southeast Asia has left little of the rainforest in its natural state. Some islands, such as the Philippines, have hardly any rainforest left. Because of this, many of the Asian rainforest species are in danger of extinction, such as the Sumastran rhino and the Vietnam pheasant. Other areas, such as Borneo, still have much of their original forest cover.

ASIAN FORESTS

Almost 40 percent of all the rainforest in Asia can be found in the Indonesian archipelago, and most of the richest mangrove forests occur along Southeast Asian coasts.

KING COBRA

The largest of all venomous, or poisonous, snakes, king cobras grow to a length of up to 18 ft (5.5 meters). They are actually shy snakes and prefer to keep well away from people. Female king cobras are the only snakes known to build a nest for their eggs.

MALAYAN TAPIR

The black and white colors of the Malayan tapir help to break up its outline so predators find it hard to see in the dark. Tapirs are shy, timid, solitary animals and come out mainly at night. They use their long trunk-like nose to pull tender shoots, buds, and fruits from rainforest plants.

MANGROVE TREES

Mangrove trees grow in salty, silty mud and have a tangle of branching roots to support them in the waterlogged ground. Special breathing roots stick up through the mud into the air to help the roots get enough oxygen. The roots also trap the mud and help to stabilize the coastline and build up new strips of land.

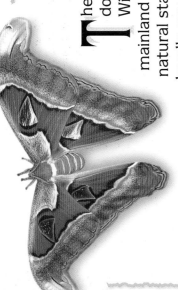

ATLAS MOTH

This is one of the largest moths in the world. It has a wingspan of up to 12 inches (30 cm) and is often mistaken for a bird as it flutters around the rainforests of Southeast Asia. Males have huge feathery antennae – the largest of any butterfly or moth – to help them pick up the scent of females among the rainforest trees.

AUSTRALASIAN RAINFORESTS

The largest expanse of rainforest in Australasia grows on the island of New Guinea. Most of it is still undisturbed and contains a mixture of Asian and Australasian plants and animals. Australasian rainforests are all that remain of a cast rainforest thain of a vast rainforest that once covered parts of this continent and Antarctica during much warmer climates millions of years ago. They are not as rich in species as other rainforests but they contain many unique forms of life.

AUSTRALASIAN FORESTS

Australasian rainforests spread up from the northeastern coast of Queensland in Australia to the island of New Guinea.

RAINBOW LORIKEET

Screeching flocks of rainbow lorikeets feed in the upper canopy, lapping up nectar and pollen from flowers with their brush-tipped tongues. They may have to fly long distances in search of flowering trees.

SPOTTED CUSCUS

Eight species of cuscus, including the spotted cuscus, occur in the rainforests of New Guinea. Cuscuses have a prehensile tail, which is mostly bald, for gripping branches. At night they feed on leaves, flowers, and insects; some species feed in the rainforest canopy, others in the understory or on the ground.

TREE KANGAROOS

Australasian rainforests do not have monkeys and apes climbing and swinging through the trees. Instead, they have tree kangaroos and a variety of marsupials, such as possums and gliders.

Tree kangaroos occur mainly on New Guinea, but two species live in Queensland rainforests. Tree kangaroos are different from ground-dwelling kangaroos because they have powerful front legs, relatively short, broad back feet, sharp claws for gripping branches, and a long, cylindrical tail. The long tail helps a tree kangaroo to balance on tree branches and also acts as a rudder when it leaps from branch to branch.

AFRICAN RAINFORESTS

THE SAME BUT DIFFERENT

Animals living in rainforests in different parts of the world have sometimes come to look the same because they have adapted to a similar lifestyle. They are different species, but because they live, feed, and survive in a similar way, their bodies look similar. This idea is called convergent evolution and some examples are the toucans of South America (below) and the hornbills of Africa (above).

African rainforests contain fewer species than the rain-forests of either America or Asia. This is because many plants and animals died out when the climate of Africa became much drier during the last Ice Age, which ended about 12,000 years ago. Most of the wildlife in Madagascar's rainforests is unique to the island because it has evolved in isolation from Africa for at least 40 million years.

RED COLOBUS MONKEY

Living in troops of 50–100 animals made up of small family groups, red colobus monkeys are active during the daytime. They feed on flowers, shoots, fruit, and leaves, leaping acrobatically from tree to tree. Unlike South American monkeys, African monkeys do not have prehensile, or gripping, tails.

GOLIATH BEETLE

The heaviest of all insects, male goliath beetles weigh from 2.5–3.5 oz (70–100 g), which is roughly three times as much as a house mouse. From the tip of the small horns to the end of the abdomen, they are up to 4 inches (11 cm) long. Females are smaller than males.

AFRICAN FORESTS

A belt of tropical rainforest grows across the center of Africa, from Cameroon and Gabon on the West African coast, to Kenya and Tanzania in East Africa. More than 80 percent of Africa's rainforest is in Central Africa. These forests spread out from small patches of forest that survived the dry African climate during the last Ice Age. In East Africa, rainforest grows mainly in mountain regions.

GREY PARROT

Noisy grey parrots whistle and shriek to each other before settling down to roost for the night in groups of 100 or more. They have remarkable powers of mimicry and captive birds can be trained to use human language as a means of communicating intelligently with people.

AMERICAN RAINFORESTS

By far the biggest area of rainforest is in the Amazon basin in South America. It is twice the size of India and ten times the size of France. About one-fifth of all the world's bird and flowering plant species and one tenth of all its mammal species live in the Amazon rainforest. Each type of tree may support more than 400 insect species.

AMERICAN RAINFORESTS

The rainforests of Central and South America range from the vast forests of the Amazon up through Central America and on to some of the islands in the Caribbean. These islands have many unusual species — some found on only one island. Hurricanes, however, often cause damage to the Caribbean rainforests. The relatively tiny rainforests of Central America are rich in species because they grow on a land bridge between two very different continents.

YELLOW ANACONDA

The yellow anaconda is one of the heaviest snakes. It is highly aquatic, hunting fish and caimans in streams and rivers. Anacondas are a type of boa and constrict their prey, squeezing it to death in their strong coils.

MORPHO BUTTERFLY

The shimmery blue colors on the wings of a male morpho butterfly help to attract females and may also serve to dazzle predators when the butterfly needs to escape. The colors are caused by the way the tiny scales on the wings reflect the light.

BALD UAKARI

With its bare face and head, long shaggy fur and a beard, the bald uakari is a strange-looking monkey indeed. The three species of uakari are the only New World monkeys to have short tails. They rarely leap, because they do not have long tails for balancing.

RAINFOREST PLANTS

Trees form the superstructure of a rainforest. Their crowns make roof gardens for perching plants, their mighty trunks support the weight of the canopy and provide climbing frames for rope-like creepers, and their roots help to hold the soil together. Rainforest trees are usually 100–160 ft (30–50 meters) tall, with slender, unbranched trunks, smooth bark, and hard wood. Their life span can be from 150 years to 1,400 years. The leaves of rainforest trees, and other rainforest plants, are often thick and leathery with pointed tips called drip tips. The rain runs quickly off these leaves and stops moss from growing and blocking out the light. A rainforest has a huge variety of trees – an area the size of a soccer field could hold as many as 200 species.

PERCHING PLANTS

To get nearer to the light, many plants perch high on the branches of the tall trees. Some of these plants, called bromeliads, make a cup-shaped container with their waxy leaves that can hold many gallons of water. Animals, like this frog, take advantage of these tree-top ponds as safe places for their young.

GROWING SPACE

One of the main problems for rainforest trees is finding a space in which to grow. Strangler figs have solved this problem by taking the place of a tree already standing.

A bird drops a strangler fig seed on a tree branch and the seed sprouts roots and branches.

The strangler's roots reach the ground and it starts to smother the host tree.

The host tree dies away, leaving the fig standing in its place.

STINKBIRDS

The hoatzin of South America smells like cow manure because its stomach is full of fermenting leaves. It is one of the few rainforest birds to feed on leaves. Leaves stay in the hoatzin's stomach for almost two days, making it too heavy to be a good flier.

BUTTRESS ROOTS

The roots of some trees spread out above the ground to form wide, flat wings called buttresses. These buttress roots may extend 16 ft (5 meters) up the trunk. They probably help to support the tall trees, but may also help the tree to feed. They spread widely and send down fine feeding roots into the soil.

CARNIVOROUS PLANTS

Pitcher plants get extra nutrients by catching and digesting insects and other small animals. Some of the pitchers rest on the ground, while others hang like lanterns along the branches of supporting trees. Some even have lids to keep out the rain. Creatures are attracted by the glistening colors and sweet nectar produced around the rim of the pitcher, but fall down the slippery walls into a pool of acidic liquid. The liquid digests the animals' bodies and the plant absorbs the nutrients they contain.

PARASITIC PLANTS

Plants need light to make food, but there is not much light on the dark forest floor. Some plants survive here by stealing their food from other plants. The biggest flower in the world, Rafflesia, is a parasitic plant like this. The body of the plant is a network of threads living inside the woody stems of a vine that hangs down from the trees and trails along the ground. The flower bud pushes its way out through the vine's bark and then expands to form a flower up to 3 ft (1 meter) across.

PLANT PARTNERS

Most flowering plants in a rainforest need pollen from another plant of the same kind in order to produce seeds. There is very little wind, so they rely on animals to transport the pollen. Highly mobile animals, such as birds, bats, and monkeys are useful for spreading seeds as they move over large areas of the forest. Flowers and seeds may sprout directly from trunks or branches to make contact more easily with bats and other large animals, without all the leaves getting in the way. Bat flowers tend to be large, pale, and smelly for finding in the dark, while bird flowers are brilliant colors because birds have good color vision. Some insects, especially ants, have more complex relationships with rainforest plants—they live right inside the plants and help them to survive.

AVOCADO BIRD

The resplendant quetzal feeds on at least 18 different species of avocado, and the trees and the birds need each other to survive. The quetzals swallow the avocado fruit whole but the hard seed passes through the bird's gut unharmed, or is regurgitated later. A new tree can grow from the seed, so the quetzal spreads avocado trees through the forest. If the avocado trees are cut down, or stop fruiting, the quetzals usually disappear from an area.

PERFUME FOR POLLEN

The bucket orchid of Central America goes to extraordinary lengths to make sure iridescent male bees carry its pollen from flower to flower. To lure the bees into its watery trap, the bucket orchid produces a perfume that the male bees use to attract female bees during courtship. While scraping perfume off the orchid's petals, the bees sometimes slip and fall down into the bucket. As it escapes, it either picks up a new load of pollen or deposits pollen it is already carrying. The pollen is the two lumps stuck to the bee's back like a yellow backpack (right).

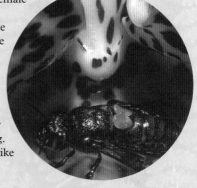

SPREADING SEEDS

Colonies of ants live inside the stems, branches, and even the leaves of several rainforest plants. In exchange for their protected nesting place, the ants provide the plants with much needed nutrients in their droppings and the remains of their insect meals. Ant plants are often epiphytes, perched high on tree branches, so they cannot get nutrients from the soil to help them grow.

The ants may also defend the plants by biting and stinging animals that try to eat them. This ant plant has holes in the surface of its swollen, prickly stem through which its ant lodgers scurry in and out of their living home. As the ants move about the forest, they help to spread the seeds of the ant plant in which they live.

GREEN FUR

The greenish tinge to the sloth's fur is provided by tiny plants called algae that live in grooves in the damp hair. Sloths never clean their fur so the algae do not get washed off, and they benefit by living high in the trees, near to the light. With green fur, sloths blend into the leafy green background of the forest so their plant hitchhikers camouflage them from predators. Another animal takes advantage of the sloth-algae relationship. A tiny moth lays it eggs in the sloth's green fur and its caterpillars seem to feed on the algae.

BEETLE MESSENGERS

To attract beetles for pollination, the *Philodendron* plant produces a powerful scent that travels great distances. The flowering spike even heats up to help the scent evaporate and disperse into the air. The beetles feed and mate inside the flower, then fly off covered with pollen to another *Philodendron* flower.

MOVING THROUGH THE TREES

In the Southeast Asian rainforests, lizards are some of the most common gliders. Their stiff gliding flaps are made of thin membranes of skin joined to their ribs. These lizards can glide for up to 50 ft (15 meters) between trees, and even change position and roll over while in the air. Gliders make easy targets for hungry birds so many are camouflaged or come out at night when it is harder for predators to see them on the move.

Even with special climbing equipment, people find it difficult and dangerous reaching the top of rainforest trees. Yet rainforest animals spend their lives swinging, climbing and gliding through the trees. Useful adaptations for these forest acrobats include long arms for swinging, tails for gripping, hanging, and balancing, and sticky toes, rough soles or long claws for extra grip. Short, rounded wings help predatory birds to twist and turn through the branches while hummingbirds and moths hover in front of flowers like jet aircraft on their small, pointed wings. Some animals glide from tree to tree instead of leaping and travel long distances with very little effort. Webs or flaps of skin increase the surface area of the body and slow down the glider's fall, like a living parachute. There is even a flying snake which can glide for distances of more than 50 meters (165 ft).

CLINGING CLAWS

The long, strong claws of a sloth work like hooks to allow the animal to spend much of its time hanging upside down from the branches of trees – even when it is asleep or dead. The claws make a rigid, fixed hook over the tree branches. The sloth's sluggish lifestyle requires very little effort and contrasts strongly with the speedy swinging of the monkeys and apes.

GRIPPING TAILS

A variety of rainforest animals, from tree porcupines and tree anteaters to kinkajous and woolly monkeys, have a special sort of tail for curling around branches like a hook. This is called a prehensile tail and it is most highly developed in South American monkeys. For some unknown reason, the monkeys of Africa and Southeast Asia have developed without this useful adaptation. Most monkeys with prehensile tails use them as a fifth limb, for holding and gathering their food, as well as for moving.

HAIRY SWINGER

With their long arms and strong fingers and toes, orangutans move easily through the trees, using their feet as well as their hands for climbing. To travel fast, they swing hand over hand, a technique called "brachiating." Older male orangs are too heavy to do this, but females and young are adept at tree-top travel, sometimes walking along branches as well as brachiating. A female orangutan has an armspan of almost 8 ft (2.4 meters) and can cover large distances quickly.

GLUED TO THE SPOT

Tree frogs such as this red-eyed tree frog have special pads under the toes that produce a sticky substance called mucus. Their sticky toes help them to grip wet leaves and other slippery and slimy surfaces as they climb through the trees.

JAGUAR

COLLARED PECCARY

GRASS, ROOTS,
BULBS, & WORMS

One of the many links between rainforest plants and animals is through their feeding habits. All food chains start with plants because they make their own food, and then the plant eaters, herbivores, in turn are eaten by meat eaters, carnivores.

HIDDEN KILLER

Curled up among the leaves of the forest floor, the gaboon viper is well camouflaged as it waits for a tasty small animal to wander past. Then it leaps out and grabs hold of its prey in a surprise attack. Gaboon vipers kill their prey by biting it with their poisonous fangs. They have the longest fangs of any snake – each one is up to 2 inches (5 cm) long. A snake's teeth are good for holding prey, but not for chopping or chewing, so snakes swallow their prey whole.

PREDATORS & PREY

Rainforest predators are mostly small animals because there are not enough large plant eaters in the forest to sustain large meat eaters. The exceptions to this are the large cats, such as the jaguar and the tiger, which hunt pigs, antelope, and deer on the forest floor. Ground-dwelling snakes also lie in wait for their prey on the forest floor, while their tree-dwelling relatives lurk among the branches. Other ground predators include troops of bush dogs in South America and sloth bears in southern India and Sri Lanka. High-level hunters include the fierce hawks and eagles that swoop down into the canopy to seize monkeys and sloths in their strong talons.

TERRIBLE TEETH

Some piranha fish, such as red-bellied piranhas, are lethal killers, carving slices of flesh from their victims with razor-sharp teeth. They have powerful jaws that snap together in a strong bite. Meat-eating piranhas have been known to attack animals as large as goats, which have fallen into the water. But all piranhas live on fruit and nuts for most of the year and some are completely vegetarian.

FELINE HUNTER

Small, agile forest cats, such as this South American margay, are skilled climbers that prey on small rodents, birds, and lizards in the trees. Most of them are nocturnal hunters and their yellow or brownish fur with spotted or striped markings gives them good camouflage. Keen sight, hearing, and smell enable them to track down their victims, which are killed with a neck bite from the sharp, pointed teeth.

SNAPPING JAWS

The caimans of Central and South America have sharper, longer teeth than their relatives the alligators. They lurk in the water, waiting to snap up fish, frogs, or thirsty animals that come down to the forest rivers for a drink. Caimans have strong, bony plates in the back and belly scales for protection against their own predators.

TONGUE ZAPPER

Insects are a major source of food for many rainforest predators, from birds and bats, to tarantula spiders and chameleons. Chameleons flick out their incredibly long tongues at lighting speed to trap insects, spiders, scorpions, and other prey on the sticky tip. To search for food, a chameleon can swivel its eyes in all directions. Their movements can be so slow that they are hardly noticeable, especially since the chameleon can change color to blend with its surroundings.

FOOD CHAIN

BENTWING BAT

INSECTS

FLOWERS

This food chain from an Australian rainforest has three links. Should any link be destroyed it will affect the rest of the chain, and all the other food chains in the large and complex food web.

DEFENSE

From armor and camouflage to weapons and poisons, rainforest animals use all kinds of defense tactics to avoid being eaten. Sometime it is possible to run, leap, fly, or glide away from a predator, but hiding or blending in with the background is often more successful. Many rainforest insects look just like leaves, twigs, or bark, and as long as they keep still they are hard to detect. Certain spiders even disguise themselves as bird droppings. Poisonous animals tend to have bright warning colors to tell predators to keep away. Some non-poisonous butterflies, such as postman butterflies, copy the colors of poisonous species to trick predators. As well as using poisons, animals may defend themselves by putting up a fight.

ANGRY PIGS

The giant forest hog is the largest wild pig and is feared by forest people for its unpredictable temper. It has well developed lower canine teeth that stick out of the sides of the mouth to form tusks. Males have larger tusks than females.

SPIDER SURVIVAL

This tarantula is trying to make itself look as frightening as possible to scare predators away. Spiders use their poisonous fangs for defense and tarantulas also flick irritating hairs at attackers. A few spiders look just like stinging insects such as wasps or ants so predators are tricked into leaving them alone. Spiders will even pretend to be dead, since predators prefer to eat living prey.

FROG POISONS

Poison arrow frogs secrete deadly poisons in their skin and are brightly colored to warn potential predators to keep away. They make some of these poisons themselves but also obtain some from their food, such as toxic insects. Their poisons are so powerful that a tiny smear is enough to ki a horse. A few Amazonian tribes use this poison on the tips of their blowpipe darts for hunting.

HIDE AND SEEK

Insects are a major source of food in the rainforest so they have developed a huge variety of unusual colors, patterns, and shapes to pretend they are not nice, tasty snacks. Dead leaves are a good disguise to adopt and leaf insects often have veins and tattered edges just like the real thing.

FALSE EYES

Some camouflaged butterflies and moths have a second line of defense if they are disturbed by a predator. They suddenly open their front wings to reveal bright colors (called flash colors) and markings on their back wings. The markings may look like the eyes of a rainforest cat or snake. This sudden display startles the predator, making them hesitate long enough for the butterfly or moth to escape.

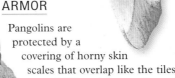

BODY ARMOR

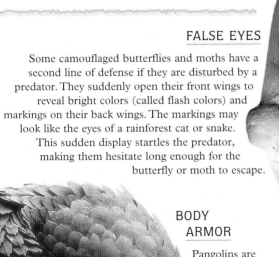

Pangolins are protected by a covering of horny skin scales that overlap like the tiles on a roof. When the pangolin curls tightly into a ball, the scales form a tough shield that only the larger cats can bite through. Pangolins eat ants and termites and their body armor helps to protect them from insect bites and stings as well as from predators.

TREE DEFENSE

To deter leaf-eating insects, the rubber tree produces a milky latex that hardens into a sticky gum. This sticks the insects' mouthparts together and prevents them from eating the tree. This latex is the raw material for making rubber. It is collected by making slanting cuts in the bark. The latex oozes slowly from the cuts and is collected in a cup fixed to the tree trunk. The bark gradually heals and the trees can be tapped again and again over a number of years.

NIGHTTIME ANIMALS

As darkness falls swiftly over the rainforest, squeaks, scratching, and rustling fill the night air. The rainforest becomes dimly lit by moonlight, flashing fireflies, or glowing fungi. As much as 80 percent of all animal activity in a rainforest takes place at night. The darkness hides animals from their enemies while the cool, moist night air suits insects and amphibians. Nighttime, or nocturnal animals, live in all parts of the rainforests. Deer, okapi, and armadillos roam the forest floor while tarsiers, bushbabies, bats, moths, and small jungle cats move through the trees. Some flowers open up specially at night so they can be pollinated by nocturnal animals. To find their way in the dark, nocturnal animals have special senses, such as huge eyes or very sensitive ears and noses. Some snakes, called pit vipers, can pick up the heat given off by birds and mammals and use this to track their prey in the dark.

BAT TRANSPORT

Rainforest bats, such this long-tongued bat, fly through the forest at night searching for nectar, fruit, and insects.

As they visit the forest flowers, bats help to spread their pollen and their seeds, so the bats and the forests help each other to survive.

SLOW MOVERS

Pottos move very slowly and deliberately through the trees so their movements go undetected. If a potto hears the slightest sound or unexpected movement, it will suddenly freeze until it feels the danger has passed. It can stay "frozen" like this for hours if necessary but the technique only works well in very thick, leafy vegetation.

NIGHT CAMOUFLAGE

The spotted markings of the clouded leopard help it to hide when it is hunting at night. Its markings help to break up the outline of its body among the leaves and branches of the forest trees. Clouded leopards hunt by pouncing from tree branches as well as by stalking prey on the ground.

TOAD INVASION

The cane toad from South America has been introduced into the rainforests of northeastern Australia. The spotted-tailed quoll (left) hunts and kills the toad. Unfortunately, the quoll is killed by the poison in the toad's skin and so the quolls' numbers have fallen drastically. The toad has no natural predators in Australia because it comes from another country, so its numbers are increasing.

NIGHT MONSTER

The rare aye-aye from Madagascar has huge ears like a bat, large eyes like an owl, and a bushy tail like a squirrel. Its most scary feature is its long, spindly middle finger. This finger is very useful to the aye-aye. It listens for the sound of insect larvae moving about inside branches and tree trunks and digs them out with its creepy finger. Unlike all other primates (monkeys, apes, lemurs, bushbabies, and humans), the aye-aye has claws instead of nails on its fingers and toes.

EYES & EARS

The huge, bat-like ears of the lesser bushbaby help it to track the movements of its insect prey in the darkness. Insects may even be snatched out of the air as they fly past.

The large eyes let in as much light as possible and there is a special layer called a 'tapetum' at the back of the eye to reflect light back into the eye. This is what makes the bushbabies' eyes shine in the dark.

COURTSHIP

In most rainforests, the weather stays the same all the time, and so there are no definite breeding seasons. The timing of courtship depends more on the reproductive cycles of the animals. Some pair up for life, while others only stay together for courtship and mating. Courtship displays in many birds are noisy, colorful affairs in which male birds show off their brightly colored feathers to impress the watching females. Females tend to have duller colors, to make them less obvious to predators when they are sitting on the nest and feeding the young. Male butterflies may be more brightly colored than the females for similar reasons. Apart from colors and display, other ways of attracting a mate include scent and sound.

PHEASANT FEATHERS

To impress a female, the male argus pheasant spreads out his stunning wing feathers to make an enormous fan. He clears a space on the forest floor and struts up and down, calling loudly to attract a female. Argus pheasants live in the rainforests of Southeast Asia.

BUTTERFLY COLORS

Some male and female butterflies, such as these morphos, are very different colors. The shimmering colors of the male may play a part in attracting a female, but the way the wings reflect ultraviolet light also seems to be important. Male butterflies use scents as well as colors to attract females and females seem to prefer the fittest males, the ones that are the strongest fliers.

BIRD OF PARADISE COURTSHIP DISPLAY

Some of the most spectacular courtship displays take place in the rainforests of New Guinea. Here, male birds of paradise perform elaborate displays; some even compete at communal display grounds, or leks, giving dazzling performances of color and sound. They often remove leaves just above their display grounds, so that a spotlight of sunshine draws attention to their spectacular dance.

Male Raggiana birds of paradise display together to show off their fabulous plumes of feathers. They shriek loudly to attract attention.

COCK-OF-THE-ROCK

On a bare patch of the Amazon forest floor, the male cock-of-the-rock displays to watching females, which are drab brown colors. He shows off by leaping into the air, bobbing his head, snapping his bill, and fanning out his feathers. He spreads his head crest forward so that it almost hides his bill. Females choose the males with the best display.

BOWERBIRDS

Instead of having bright, colorful feathers, male bowerbirds attract females by building an elaborate shelter, called a bower. Each bowerbird builds a different shape of bower from twigs woven together and decorated with colorful objects, such as shells, fruits, bones, pebbles, feathers, and flowers. Things thrown away by people, such as old bottle tops, sometimes end up decorating these bowers.

SCENTED MESSAGES

Female and male tigers live apart and only come together for mating. When a tigress is ready to mate, she leaves scent marks along the paths in her territory. This tigress is leaving a scented message for a male tiger by rubbing scent glands on her face against tree bark. She also roars loudly to attract the attention of nearby males.

PARROT COURTSHIP

Before they mate, most male parrots display to the females by bowing, hopping, strutting, flicking their wings, and wagging their tails. They may also feed the female regurgitated food.

In many species, the brightly colored irises of the eyes are expanded – this is called eye blazing. Most parrots are monogamous and males and females often pair for life. They reinforce the bond between them by preening each other's feathers and feeding each other.

LIFE CYCLE OF AN OWL BUTTERFLY

A butterfly goes through four stages in its life cycle: egg, caterpillar, pupa, and adult. In the warm climate of a tropical rainforest, a butterfly develops quickly and may complete its whole life cycle in just a few weeks.

Ribs and tough coating on the eggs keep them from drying out.

Young caterpillars have a green skin; older ones have a brown skin. Their function is to eat and grow bigger.

Inside the pupa, the caterpillar changes into a butterfly.

The role of the adult butterfly is reproduction and dispersal.

FROG TRANSPORT

Poison dart frogs usually lay their eggs on a leaf or a small area of ground that they have carefully cleaned. One or both parents visit or guard the eggs until they hatch into tadpoles. Then the parent encourages the tadpoles to wriggle up on to its back and carries them to a stream or a pool of water among the leaves of a forest plant. Up to 35 tadpoles are carried in this way. The tadpoles do not fall off the adult's back because they are held there by a sticky secretion that is only broken down when it is underwater.

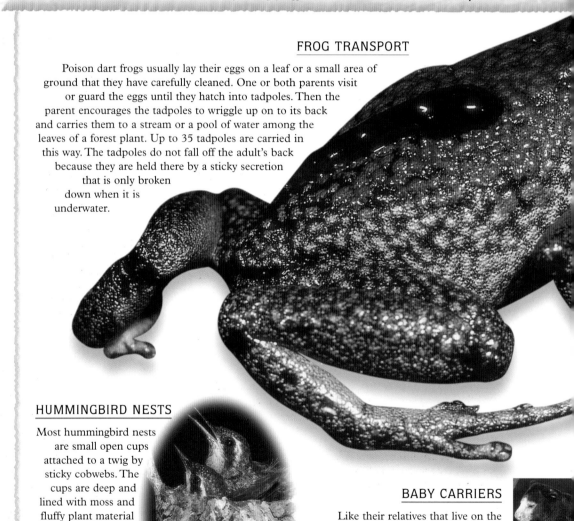

HUMMINGBIRD NESTS

Most hummingbird nests are small open cups attached to a twig by sticky cobwebs. The cups are deep and lined with moss and fluffy plant material to keep the eggs and young birds warm. Even after leaving the nest, the fledgling hummingbird is fed by the mother for as long as 20–40 days.

BABY CARRIERS

Like their relatives that live on the ground, mother tree kangaroos have pouches to carry their young. The babies are born at a very early stage of their development. They crawl up to the pouch, fasten on to a teat, and spend several months there, completing their development. Inside the pouch, the baby is warm and safe and can feed whenever it is hungry.

NESTS, EGGS & YOUNG

Although there is plenty of food and a variety of places to nest in a rainforest, animals still have to compete for safe nesting sites and protect their eggs and young from predators. The warm temperatures help the young to develop and survive the early, vulnerable stages of the life cycle, but the constant rain can make life miserable. Birds protect their eggs and young inside nests or tree holes while marsupial mothers, such as tree kangaroos or possums, carry their young around with them for months in furry pouches. Even tarantulas guard their eggs until they hatch. But mammals, such as monkeys, cats, and bats, take the greatest care of their young, teaching them how to feed, hunt, and survive in the forest.

STRIPES & SPOTS

Adult Brazilian tapirs are a plain brown color but their young have spots and stripes on their fur. This helps to camouflage them so they blend into the background as they move through the light and shade of the rainforest. The markings also break up the outline of the young animal's body so it is harder to see.

CLINGING BABIES

A female orangutan usually gives birth to a single baby every three to six years. The baby rides on its mother's back or clings to her fur as she swings through the trees and sleeps in the same nest at night. Baby orangutans are totally dependent on their mothers for the first 18 months of their lives. Mother orangutans do not mate again until their young are at least three years old so a female may only have two or three babies during her lifetime.

LIVING TOGETHER

Social rainforest animals help each other to spot predators, find food, and defend their young. In mammal societies where individuals live a long time, experienced older members of a group can help younger, inexperienced animals and teach them various survival skills. Mammal societies often have a "dominance hierarchy," where some are more important or high ranking than others. Insect societies are highly organized, with groups of individuals carrying out different tasks.

ANT GARDENS

Colonies of leafcutter ants from Central American rainforests grow their own food in an underground nest. Worker ants bite off pieces of leaf and carry them back to the nest. Here the leaves are chewed into small pieces, fertilized with the ants' droppings, and used to provide a compost for growing fungi. The ants eat the fungus once it has grown. In some forests, leafcutter ants may eat over 15 percent of all the leaves grown.

TERMITE TOWERS

Tiny insects called termites build the equivalent of insect skyscrapers on the forest floor. These towers are built of tiny pieces of mud and saliva and take many years to build. Millions of termites live in almost total darkness inside each tower. The queen termite lays the eggs; the workers look after the eggs and young, and gather food; and soldier termites defend the nest.

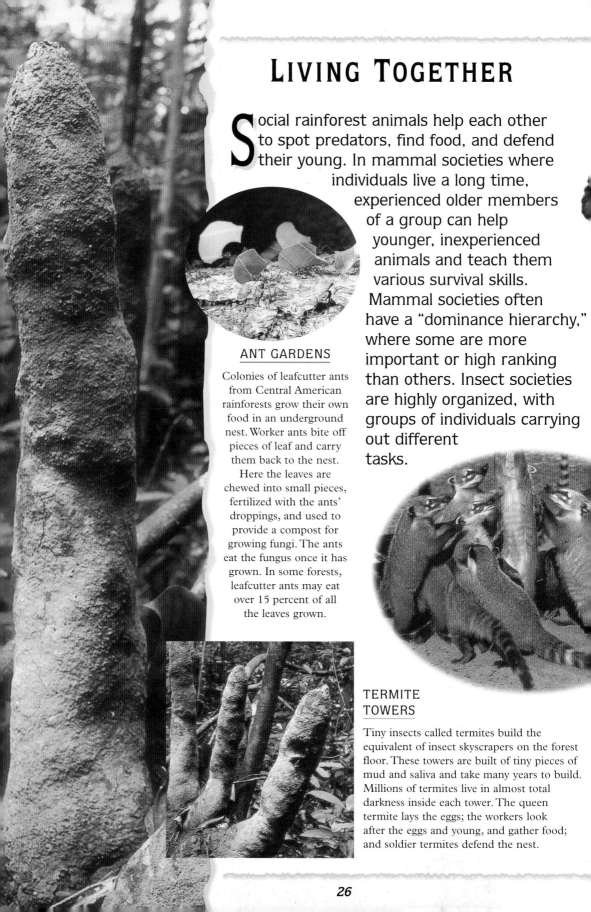

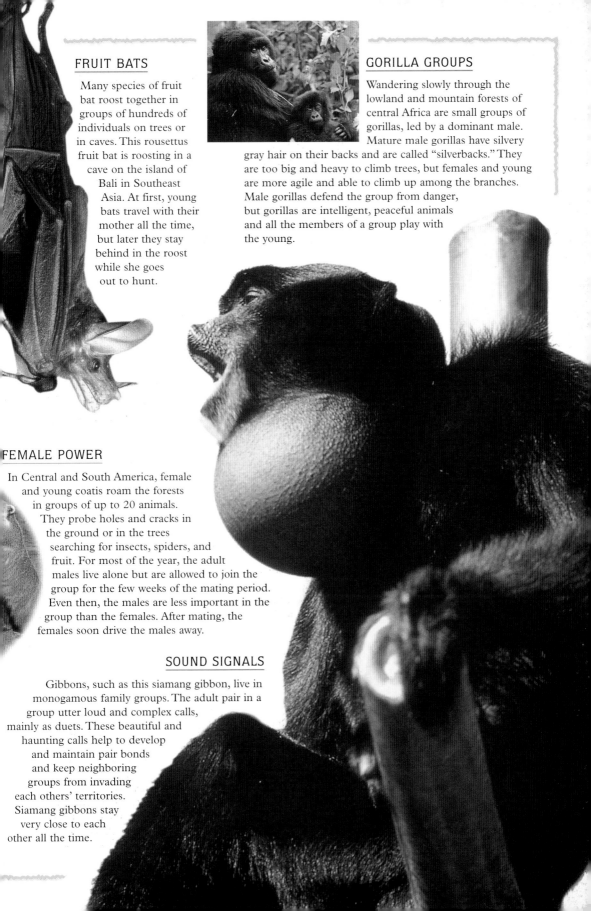

FRUIT BATS

Many species of fruit bat roost together in groups of hundreds of individuals on trees or in caves. This rousettus fruit bat is roosting in a cave on the island of Bali in Southeast Asia. At first, young bats travel with their mother all the time, but later they stay behind in the roost while she goes out to hunt.

GORILLA GROUPS

Wandering slowly through the lowland and mountain forests of central Africa are small groups of gorillas, led by a dominant male. Mature male gorillas have silvery gray hair on their backs and are called "silverbacks." They are too big and heavy to climb trees, but females and young are more agile and able to climb up among the branches. Male gorillas defend the group from danger, but gorillas are intelligent, peaceful animals and all the members of a group play with the young.

FEMALE POWER

In Central and South America, female and young coatis roam the forests in groups of up to 20 animals. They probe holes and cracks in the ground or in the trees searching for insects, spiders, and fruit. For most of the year, the adult males live alone but are allowed to join the group for the few weeks of the mating period. Even then, the males are less important in the group than the females. After mating, the females soon drive the males away.

SOUND SIGNALS

Gibbons, such as this siamang gibbon, live in monogamous family groups. The adult pair in a group utter loud and complex calls, mainly as duets. These beautiful and haunting calls help to develop and maintain pair bonds and keep neighboring groups from invading each others' territories. Siamang gibbons stay very close to each other all the time.

PEOPLE OF THE RAINFOREST

For thousands of years, the world's rainforests have been home to groups of people who have a deep and sensitive understanding of the forests. Their knowledge of the rainforest's plants and animals, and their ability to use a wide range of foods and natural medicines, are the keys to their survival. Population densities have never been high.

Some rainforest people cultivate small patches of forest in a form of shifting cultivation. Unfortunately, as forests are cleared for their timber or their land, the homes of forest people are destroyed, or they are killed by diseases, such as influenza and measles, introduced by settlers from outside the forest.

NEW GUINEA HIGHLANDERS

The New Guinea highlanders decorate themselves in magnificent costumes for special occasions and perform complicated dances. They paint their faces and bodies in vivid colors. The pattern often has something to do with religious beliefs and ancestral spirits.

HUNTING WEAPONS

This Mentawai man from Indonesia is carrying his bow and arrow along with some stripped bark. To capture monkeys, birds, and other prey high in the canopy, rainforest hunter-gatherers use poisoned arrows or darts. The poisons used come from plant juices or the skin of poisonous tree frogs, and sometimes hunters have to wait for hours before the animal dies and falls out of the trees.

PYGMIES

The pygmies of Africa are adapted physically as well as culturally to their way of life as hunter-gatherers in the forest. Their small size makes it easier to move about in the undergrowth and they have a light, muscular build that is well suited to tree climbing. Some tribes of pygmies seem to be completely at home in the tree tops, often climbing to reach the nests of wild bees to collect the honey. A small bird called a honeyguide often leads the hunters to a hive. The hunter helps the bird by opening the hive and leaves it a meal of beeswax as a reward.

NUMBERS OF PEOPLE

A large area of rainforest can support only a few hundred people – the population density of the Mbuit pygmies is only about one person for every 1.5 square miles (4 square kilometers), and an individual band may range over as much as 500 square miles (1,300 square kilometers) in their search for food. Rainforest peoples are spread thinly through the forest. Some build houses for a time; many families may live in the same house.

FOREST TRANSPORT

In dense forest, it is easier to travel along rivers than to move through the undergrowth. Dugout canoes are often used for transport, even today, but making them takes a long time. A tree has to be felled and then cut and hollowed out with an axe. Pieces of wood called stretchers are placed across the canoe to prevent it from warping. When the canoe is finished, a fire is lit underneath and inside the canoe to harden and seal the wood.

SHIFTING CULTIVATION

Also called "slash-and-burn," shifting cultivation is well suited to the poor soils of a rainforest. The people cut down and burn a small area of forest so the nutrients in the plants enrich the soil for a while and weeds are destroyed. Then they plant seeds, and as the crops grow, the plot needs constant weeding, since weeds grow well in the warm, wet conditions. Eventually, the weeds overcome the crops and the goodness in the soil is used up so the people move on to another patch of forest. Cultivated areas are left to lie fallow, or rest and recover, for between 8 and 20 years. Shifting cultivation does not cause any lasting harm to the forest.

CEREMONIES

Many rainforest people paint their bodies with colorful dyes and use feathers, flowers, and other natural materials to make jewelry. Men, such as this Cofan Indian from Ecuador, are sometimes the only ones allowed to wear full ceremonial costume. There are strong traditions of dance and ceremony and special occasions such as weddings, funerals, and harvests are marked by dances and feasts.

Protecting the Rainfores[t]

Rainforests have taken millions of years to turn into the complex environments that they are today. They are very fragile because every part depends on every other part. Unfortunately, most rainforests are in poor, developing countries, which need to make money from timber; mineral resources, such as iron, copper, or uranium; or cash-crops, such as coffee, cocoa, or bananas. Forest clearance causes many problems such as soil erosion, floods, droughts, extinction of species, and disturbance of forest people. About half of all the rainforests in the world have already been cut down and an area about the size of a soccer field disappears every second. Much more could be done to save the world's rainforests. Timber companies could replace the trees they cut down, or grow plantations of valuable rainforest trees. Trade in rare animal species could be controlled more effectively, and more large areas of rainforest preserved as national parks.

TIMBER!

With chain saws, backhoes, and powerful machinery, logging companies can clear huge areas of rainforest in a frighteningly short time. It takes several hundred years for a rainforest tree to grow taller than an electrical tower and only a few minutes for a man to chop it down with a chain saw. Roads have to be built to get the machinery into the forest and, as the valuable timber trees are scattered throughout the forest, great holes have to be torn in the forest to reach each one. Loggers usually destroy three times as many trees as they harvest.

OUT INTO THE WILD

The numbers of endangered species can be increased by breeding them in captivity and then releasing them back into the wild. This is not a simple process because the animals have never been in a natural rainforest and have to learn how to survive. Scientists have fitted these tamarins with radio collars so they can follow their movements through the forest. In 1908, only about 100 golden lion tamarins survived in the wild, but conservation work has now increased numbers to about 400.

MEDICINAL PLANTS

These Antanosy girls are holding a rosy periwinkle plant, which is used for making drugs to treat certain types of childhood leukemia and Hodgkin's disease, a form of cancer. The plant grows in the rapidly disappearing rainforests of Madagascar and may soon become an endangered species. Many other rainforest plants could contain useful drugs but they may become extinct before they are discovered. Twenty percent of all drugs contain extracts of rainforest plants, yet only one percent of rainforest plants have been tested.

RAINFOREST RESEARCH

Although rainforest people have a vast storehouse of knowledge about plants and animals in the forest, scientists also need to collect data to back up conservation projects. Millions of species need to be identified and the complex web of life better understood to work out how best to preserve the rainforests for the future. Since it is difficult to travel through the forest, some researchers float over the forest in airships or take samples from the canopy using tree-top rafts.

PROTECTED SPECIES

Large sums of money can be made from the trade in endangered animals and plants. International laws aim to protect rare species but it is often difficult to enforce the laws. The jaguar is fully protected under the CITES (Convention on International Trade in Endangered Species) but there is still illegal trade in its skin. Often the people who catch the animals make very little money from the trade, with the traders making most of the profit. If people refuse to buy goods made from protected species, this will help to limit further trade.

FIND OUT MORE

Useful Addresses

To find out more about rainforests, or the protection of rainforest wildlife, here are some organizations that may be able to help.

CARIBBEAN CONSERVATION CORPORATION
4424 NW 13th Street, Suite A1
Gainesville, FL 32609
(352) 373-6441, ccc.@cccturtle.org

FRIENDS OF THE EARTH
1025 Vermont Avenue, NW, 3rd Floor
Washington, DC, 20005
(202) 783-7400, foe@foe.org

RAINFOREST ACTION
221 Pine Street, Suite 500, San Francisco, CA 94104
(415) 398-4404

RAINFOREST ALLIANCE
65 Bleecker Street, New York, NY 10012
(212) 677-1900 or 888-MY EARTH

SIERRA CLUB ENVIRONMENTAL EDUCATION
85 Second Street, Second Floor
San Francisco, CA 94105-3441
(415) 977-5500

TROPICAL RAINFOREST COALITION
21730 Stevens Creek Blvd., Suite 102
Cupertino, CA 95014
(408) 496-9412

WORLD WILDLIFE FUND
1250 24th Street NW, Washington, DC, 20037
1-800-225-5993

Useful websites

RAINFOREST ACTION NETWORK
http://www.ran.org

YOUNG PEOPLE'S TRUST FOR THE ENVIRONMENT AND NATURE CONSERVATION
http://www.btinternet.com

First edition for the United States, its territories and dependencies, Canada and the Philippine Republic,
published 1999 by Barron's Educational Series, Inc.
Original edition copyright © 1999 by Ticktock Publishing, Ltd.
U.S. edition copyright © 1999 by Barron's Educational Series, Inc.
All rights reserved. No part of this book may be reproduced in any form, by photostat, microfilm, xerography, or any other means, or incorporated into any information retrieval system, electronic or mechanical, without the written permission of the copyright owner.
All inquiries should be addressed to: Barron's Educational Series, Inc., 250 Wireless Boulevard, Hauppauge, New York 11788,
http://www.barronseduc.com
Library of Congress Catalog Card No. 98-74865
International Standard Book No. 0-7641-0642-2
Printed in Hong Kong
987654321

Picture Credits: t=top, b=bottom, c=center, l=left, r=right, OFC=outside front cover, OBC=outside back cover, IFC=inside front cover

B&C Alexander; 28/29c, 29cr. Bruce Coleman Limited; 12/13b, 14tr, 20tl. Colorific; 3c. Jacana; 2tl, 6bl, 7tr, 7br, 8cr, 10/11t, 11tr, 12tl, 13r, 14bl, 17tr, 18c, 18/19c, 19b, 21br, 26/27c, 27b, 31br & OFC. Oxford Scientific Films; IFC, 12br, 19tc, 22tl, 24br, 26tl. Planet Earth Pictures; OFC (main pic), 2l & 2bl, 3/4b, 3tr, 3/4t, 4/5t, 4/5c, 4/5b, 5br, 6br, 6c, 6tr, 7bl, 8tl, 8tr, 8c, 8br, 9t, 9c, 9cr, 10l, 10tl, 11c, 11b, 14/15b, 15br & OBC, 16tl, 16bl, 17c & 32, 17b, 18tl, 18bl, 19tr, 20bl, 20cr, 21tl, 21c, 21tr, 22c, 22cl, 22/23ct, 23tr, 23cl, 23br, 24/25c, 24bl, 25tr, 25br, 26l & 26bl, 26/27t, 27t, 28tl, 28bl, 29br & OBC, 30tl, 30bl, 30/31c, 31tr. P.I.X; 15t. Tony Stone; 29cl.

Every effort has been made to trace the copyright holders and we apologize in advance for any unintentional omissions.
We would be pleased to insert the appropriate acknowledgment in any subsequent edition of this publication.

BARRON'S